THE TODDLER'S POTTY BOOK

Written by Alida Allison

Illustrations by Henri Parmentier

PRICE STERN SLOAN

Los Angeles

We would like to express our gratitude to
Beatrice L. Cole and Marion McMillan
of SC Productions for their help and encouragement.

Toodler's Potty Book

Copyright © 1984, 1979, 1978 Alida Allison
Illustrations copyright © 1984 Price Stern Sloan, Inc.
Published by Price Stern Sloan, Inc.,
A member of The Putnam & Grosset Group, New York, New York

15 14 13 12 11

A Very Important Note to Parents

This book is special. We know, because when our children were ready to outgrow diapers, we went looking for a book like this and couldn't find one.

THE TODDLER'S POTTY BOOK is designed to help your child literally get the picture of potty training, through drawings that he or she will understand and love. The text provides a positive, supportive framework for you to use in communicating this primary learning experience.

Visualization of a concept or behavior makes it easier to understand by establishing a mental pattern. The pictures in this book are designed to create a pattern of confidence and pride in your child's ability to function "like a big kid."

We suggest that you take a look at your bathroom from your child's perspective. Adult-size fixtures are unmanageable for children; purchase of a child-size toilet will help your child feel more secure. So will a footstool, which should also be useful at toothbrushing time.

We also suggest that you use the bibliography at the end of the book. Being informed about toilet training will help *you* feel confident, too.

Getting your child used to the toilet and to having dry pants is your primary focus. Learning to flush can come later.

You and your youngster are special. Use whatever functional terms you prefer; the words are not as important as the quality of the experience you share.

Alida Allison

It sure feels good to
have dry pants.
Wet pants are no fun.

I can see that daddy's
pants are dry.
Mommy uses the potty so her
pants are dry too.

This is my potty.

I'm a big kid.
I can use the potty.

Hurray! I did it!
I used the potty.

Mommy and Daddy
are so happy.
Gramma and Grampa
are happy, too.

Everybody's happy.

I feel big and proud and dry.

Wanna' know a secret?

Using the toilet is easy!

Dry pants feel great!

Now I'm a big kid, too!

How about you?

Bibliography

(Pages relating to toilet training are noted.)

Toilet Train in Less Than a Day, Nathan Azrin and Richard Foxx, Pocket Books, New York, 1976

Tips for Toddlers, Brooke McKamy Beebe, Dell Books, New York, 1983, pgs. 31-47

Parents Book of Toilet Training, Joanna Cole, Parents Magazine Press, New York, 1983

How to Parent, Fitzhugh Dodson, Signet, New York, 1970, pgs. 132-143

The Early Childhood Years, Theresa Kaplan and F. Kaplan, Putnam, New York, 1983, pgs. 72-74, 118-119

Practical Parenting Toilet Training, Vicki Lansky, Bantam Books, New York, 1984

The Mother to Mother Baby Care Book, Barbara Sills and Jeanne Henry, Avon, New York, 1980, pgs. 297-309

Baby and Child Care, Benjamin Spock, Simon and Schuster, New York, 1977, revised, pgs. 286-296

Your Child from One to Twelve, Signet, New York, 1970, pgs. 37-43